REMEMBER MR. BEAR

Written by Chizuko Kuratomi
Illustrated by Kozo Kakimoto

MACDONALD: LONDON

High on a mountain a big shaggy bear lived all by himself.
He had no friends and he felt lonely. "I will go down to the
town in the valley," he thought. So he put on his best clothes
and off he went.

When he arrived in Rabbit Town
it was chock-a-block with traffic,
Buses and cars roared past
on either side of him.
Everyone seemed to be in such a hurry.
He thought they must all have
very important things to do.
The main street frightened him.

Suddenly the traffic stopped with a screech of brakes.
Mr. Bear did not understand about the red traffic lights.
He felt sure something had gone wrong.
Perhaps, he thought, the engines had got stuck

because they had worked so hard.
Perhaps a helpful push
would put everything right.
He pushed. You can see what happened.

Then he found a quiet house
whose door stood wide open.
He knocked and took off his hat
ready to bow politely,
but there was nobody inside.

Mr. Bear had come
a long way
and felt very tired.
He put a lot of little chairs
in two rows,
lay down on them
and fell asleep.
But he was too big
for the chairs
and most of them
broke.

He did not know that the house
was a rabbit kindergarten
and he had walked into
one of the classrooms.
When the little rabbits
came back to school after lunch
they could hardly believe
their eyes.

"Who is he?" they said.
"How huge he is."
"Look how many chairs
are broken."

At first the rabbits
were frightened of Mr. Bear,
but when they had had
a good look at him
they did not feel frightened
any more. Some of them began
to make a drawing of him
on the blackboard
and the squeak
of their chalks
woke him up.

He was so upset
about the chairs.
"Towns seem to be
such odd places,"
he said to the teacher.
"Nothing here seems to fit me."

Out in the street again, Mr. Bear found a gang of rabbits mending the road. It looked easy enough to use a pickaxe

and he thought he would help them.
He did so want to be useful to somebody.

Mr. Bear was good at digging holes.
He lifted the pickaxe high in the air
and brought it down
with all his might—

—straight into
the water main.
Water shot up
all over
everything.
It was like
a fountain.

"Hey, stop that," shouted the rabbit
in charge of the digging.
"What do you think you are doing?"
But Mr. Bear looked so upset
that the rabbit felt sorry for him.
"Cheer up," he said,
"you did your best.
It was kind of you
to try to help."

It was too late; Mr. Bear had decided to go home.
He had brought sacks of presents
for the friends he hoped to make.
He left them all for the rabbits to share.
They watched him trudge away
and waved until he was
out of sight.

They never forgot Mr. Bear in Rabbit Town. He was so
big and so strange and so frightening—and yet he was
nice and gave everyone presents. He had made all the
animals of Rabbit Town his friends. They even put up
a statue of him/and the little rabbits still sing:

Mr. Bear, Mr. Bear,
No one stronger anywhere
Big and slow, big and slow,
Tried so hard but didn't know
Big and dim, big and dim,
But all of us were fond of him.

© Shiko-Sha Co. Ltd., Tokyo, September 1966
© Text, Macdonald & Co. (Publishers) Ltd., 1967
First published in Great Britain in 1967 by
Macdonald & Co. (Publishers) Ltd.,
49 Poland Street, London W.1.
Printed in Japan by Shiko-Sha Co. Ltd., Tokyo

Second impression 1973

ISBN 0 356 01383 9